Off to a great start!

How To Fly for Kids!

by Natalie Windsor

Illustrated by Joe Azar

CorkScrew Press

LOS ANGELES

Distributed by The Globe Pequot Press

Published by CorkScrew Press, Inc.
4470 Sunset Boulevard, Suite 234
Los Angeles, California 90027

This book contains information based on current U.S. law and U.S. airline policies, which may not apply internationally. Neither the author nor the publisher is engaged in rendering legal, medical or other professional advice, and is not responsible for any loss or damage resulting from reliance on the contents of this book.

Distributed by The Globe Pequot Press
P.O. Box 833 ◆ Old Saybrook, CT 06475-0833
Distributed in Canada by General Publishing, Don Mills, Ontario.

Library of Congress Cataloging-in-Publication Data
Windsor, Natalie.
        How to fly — for kids! : your fun-in-the-sky airplane companion /
    [by Natalie Windsor].
            p.   cm.
        ISBN 0-944042-33-3
        1. Aeronautics, Commercial—Juvenile literature.
    [1. Aeronautics, Commercial. 2. Airplanes. 3. Airports.]
    I. Title.
    HE9776.W56 1994 387.7—dc20   94-24625

For single-copy orders, see page 143, or call 1-800-243-0495.
For quantity discounts, please write to the distributor.

Captain Wrightway and *Sky Ryder* are trademarks of CorkScrew Press, Inc.

Other trademarks used in this book are property of various trademark owners.

Printed in the U.S.A.

10 9 8 7 6 5 4 3 2 1

To enjoy the adventure of flying, you only need four things: courage, good manners, a terrific busy bag, and someone to hug when you land.

Sincere thanks to the experts and contributors who helped make this book as factual as it is fun:

Bonnie Teixeira, Educational Consultant; Arthur Lampel, J.D.; Jon A. Pace, hypnotherapist; Reed Price, M.A.; Dr. Elaine D. Nemzer, child psychiatrist; Dr. Anita Lampel, child psychologist; Bernard Chasman; Ellen Goldberg; Pat Rodney, flight attendant, Southwest Airlines; Marina Biallo, psychotherapist; Ada Hedland; Lisa Beezley; Agnes J. Huff, Ph.D.; Timothy Kelly, U.S. Department of Transportation; Patrick Walsh, American Airlines Flight Service Manager, DFW; Jill Reis, physical therapist; Gale Sloan, American Airlines Flight Service Manager, DFW; Barry Brayer, FAA; Elly Brekke, FAA, Pat Jorgenson, U.S. Geological Survey, Ilan Migdali, L.Ac.; Greg Doss, Public Affairs Specialist, U.S. Customs Service; Neal Marks; Beth Watschke, teacher; Nancy Neckelmann, teacher; and Ro & Shel.

And special thanks to our great team of *How To Fly* Test Pilots

Joshua Lampel, 7; Adriana Huff, 13; Jordan Karney, 10; Noah Levin, 10; Christian Neckelmann, 7; Matthew Neckelmann, 5; and Miss Watschke's First and Second Grade Class, Kellogg Polytechnic Elementary School, Pomona, CA.

Cover design by
Ken Niles
Ad Infinitum, Santa Monica, CA

Introduction

We are so lucky to be able to fly!

Our grandparents' grandparents were able to see only small corners of the world. Back then, traveling long distances took weeks and months. Many people had to kiss their families goodbye forever, so they could travel to places that we can reach now in just a few hours.

Flying is best when you're prepared for it and you understand it — and when you enjoy the time you spend on the plane.

So get out your pencil, start your imagination and get set to take off on a terrific adventure.

Have a great flight!

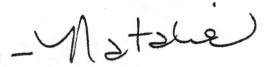

Welcome Aboard

BOARDING PASS TICKET TO ADVENTURE **SEAT 1A**

Here's practically everything you need
to have a fun, safe, entertaining airplane trip!

Contents

Before Every Trip

What should I bring in my luggage?

It might sound funny, but a calendar makes it easy to pack your suitcase. Just count how many days you'll be away, then fill in each activity box on page 15. You can be sure you've packed all the right things for your trip.

What should I wear?

Start with your feet, then dress the rest of you. Play day on Wednesday? Pack athletic shoes, a shirt and shorts or jeans. Ski trip on Friday? Heavy socks, gloves and warm clothes. Party or wedding on Saturday? Dress shoes and nice clothes.

Under everything

Pack a pair of clean socks and underwear for each day. If your trip will take more than a week, pack seven or eight pairs, and plan to get them washed.

Night stuff

Pack your slippers and whatever you need to sleep in. Bring a robe if you're going someplace where you want to be warm or more private.

Meet Captain Wrightway. He'll pilot you through the entire book.

Lookin' good

Be sure to bring your comb, toothbrush and toothpaste. Pack soap and shampoo in a recloseable plastic bag so they won't leak on your other things.

Personal stuff

Little kids often have a favorite stuffed animal or blanket, older kids might have a special photo, book or toy. Packing something you especially like lets you bring a little bit of home with you.

Captain Wrightway's 'Think Ahead' Packing Guide

EXPECTING...	THEN BRING...
➤ Rainy weather?	Umbrella, raincoat.
➤ Cold weather?	Sweater or jacket.
➤ Allergy sneezing?	Extra tissues.
➤ Boring relatives?	Extra books and games.
➤ To be outdoors?	Sunglasses, sunscreen, bug spray.
➤ To buy lots of things?	An extra backpack.
➤ To go swimming?	Bathing suit, flip-flops.
➤ To write postcards?	Postage stamps & addresses.
➤ To stay several places?	Nothing you'd hate to lose.

My

Sample Packing Guide

Here's how to remember to pack everything you need for your trip.

Thurs day

Activity _Travel_

I need,
a magazine,
a plane ticket,
and some food
and
a toothbrush
PJ's
A hat
and a pair
Of Shoes.

_____ day

Activity_____

_____ day

Activity_____

Packing Guide

Write or draw the things YOU need to pack for your trip.

_____day Activity_____	_____day Activity_____	_____day Activity_____

If you need more days, draw your own guide on a separate sheet of paper.

Stuff I might need to carry on

One of the best parts about flying is you get to use the time any way you want — ALMOST. Tap dancing, kite flying and yodeling are out, but there's plenty you CAN do. So pack yourself an easy-to-carry busy bag filled with your favorite things.

Stuff I might need with me:

- ➤ Money — including coins for phone calls
- ➤ Chewing gum to help my ears pop
- ➤ Sports bottle — ask the flight attendant for water
- ➤ Snack food that isn't messy
- ➤ Tissues

Fun stuff I'll want with me:

- ➤ Books
- ➤ Magazines or comics
- ➤ Diary or journal
- ➤ Easy-to-carry games
- ➤ Pencils, crayons and paper

Stuff that's NOT okay to bring with me:

➢ Anything that smells
➢ Anything really noisy
➢ Anything really big
➢ Anything sloppy or wet
➢ Anything with lots of little parts to lose
➢ Anything that looks or sounds like a gun or weapon

Sometimes you can bring hand-held computer games, or a personal stereo — WITH HEADPHONES — if you use them only during the times they are allowed. Ask an adult to check with the airline to see if it's okay.

TO GATE

What I need to know about other people

What are so many people doing at the airport?

Airports are very busy places. It's not like going to a friend's house or the mall — people don't just hang out. At airports, everybody has a reason to be there.

You'll see lots of people rushing around. They're meeting other people, racing to get on planes, or arriving from faraway places. You'll also see people hug and kiss as they say hello or goodbye to family and friends. Other people work there selling things like magazines and hot dogs.

But a few people go to the airport for bad reasons: they want what you have. Travelers who are rushing or hugging or kissing aren't paying much attention to their stuff, and robbers love that. Luggage, money — even backpacks with personal belongings inside — all give robbers their reason to go to the airport. So YOU have to be very smart and alert.

Keep a close watch on your things. Never walk away and leave them.

Where to put your stuff

When you're waiting in the airport, the best place for your carry-on bag or backpack is on your lap — or on the floor between your feet. NEVER WALK AWAY AND LEAVE IT!

If you're flying by yourself and any airline employees have been asked to watch out for you, don't give them hassles or headaches. Their job is to protect you and see that you get on your plane safely. So let them escort you. Wandering off isn't funny — it's dangerous and dumb.

Some people are naturally nice — and they're just chatting with you to keep you company. But if somebody who doesn't work for the airline comes up to you and wants to start a conversation, be extra alert. If a stranger seems "wrong" to you, or asks about who's meeting you, or asks about your money — run to the adult in charge or yell for help!

It's about money, honey!

You don't need money to make a collect call home in an emergency. See the inside back cover to find out how.

Everyone likes having money. But to keep it, you've got to know how to hang onto it. Put a big dollar sign ($) in front of every statement you think is true:

___1 The best places to keep your money are in shirt pockets with flaps, front pockets in pants, fanny packs turned to the front, or in your shoes.

___2 Anyone who would rip-off a kid's money is a slimy rat-faced hairball (but there ARE some slimy rat-faced hairballs out there).

___3 Money grows on trees.

___4 It's smart to separate your money into several safe places: a couple of spending dollars in one pocket, coins in another pocket, and larger bills in a secret place.

___5 It's nobody's business how much money you have. In fact, if a stranger comes up and asks about your money — run or holler for help.

___6 Once you're on the plane, sodas and snacks are free!

For the correct answers, turn to page 129.

Circle the **10** money mistakes and baggage blunders:

The answers are on page 129.

Last-Minute Pre-Flight Checklist

Before you leave the house, make sure your busy bag is set up so you can get to things easily on the plane.

☐ Do all my bags — including my carry-on — have filled-out luggage tags?

☐ Is my money hidden in several safe places?

☐ Do I have coins, in case I need to make a phone call?

☐ Where's my airline ticket?

☐ If I'm bringing a watch, am I wearing it?

☐ Do I have my sunglasses and umbrella?

☐ Did somebody call the airline to make sure the plane is leaving on time?

☐ Should an adult make a last-minute call to the person picking me up?

☐ Is my busy bag complete? Read page 16.

☐ Have I filled out the front inside cover of this book?

If your parent says it's okay, use bright plastic tape or stickers to decorate your suitcases. This helps you find your bags later.

At The Airport

Meet Sky Ryder!

The only superhero who needs a plane to fly!

Meet Sky Ryder. Sky used to be scared of flying by himself, but he quickly realized there was no reason to be afraid. He learned he could get anything he really needed on a plane, because the crew members were friendly and always there to help him. Sky also discovered that knowing what was going on — and preparing for it — made his flights happier and easier.

Sky has become a kind of superhero, because he's helped so many kids who fly by themselves. He wants to share valuable secrets with you, to make YOUR flight happy and easy. Look for him to give you tips throughout the book.

Airport Adventures

What's my luggage doing right now?

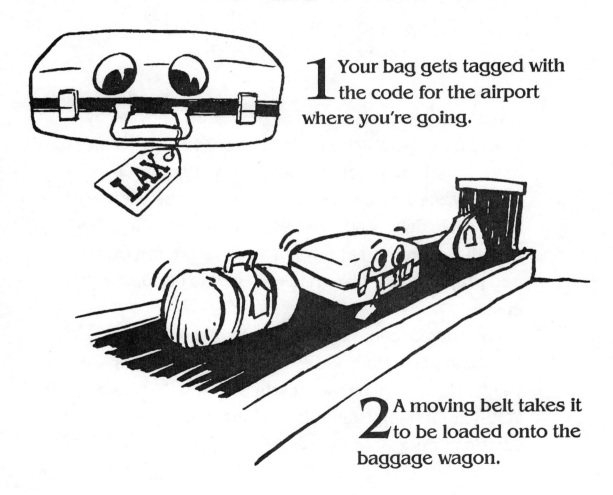

1 Your bag gets tagged with the code for the airport where you're going.

2 A moving belt takes it to be loaded onto the baggage wagon.

3 The baggage wagon then takes it to the plane.

4 From some window seats, you might see your own luggage being loaded into the plane's baggage hold.

5 At the end of your flight, your bag gets unloaded and transported to baggage claim, where you can pick it up.

Purse & Luggage Guts

If there's time, you can see inside everyone else's luggage on the X-ray monitor!

Just before the gates where people board the planes, security checkpoints make sure passengers don't bring dangerous things with them. Airlines have very big lists of what's not okay to bring on a plane — they're not just looking for weapons.

To make sure everybody is super-safe and completely honest, security guards put everyone's carry-on bags through a big X-ray machine. Then the people walk through a magnetic arch, designed to sound off when metal things go through them.

What should you do?

Your job is to put your stuff down flat on the X-ray machine's moving belt, and then walk under the magnetic arch. If you hurry, and if you ask the uniformed guard, you can see the X-ray of what's in your bag. If you have enough time, and you're not bugging anybody, you can hang around there a little longer and see other people's purse and briefcase guts on the screen!

Watch for the shadowy X-ray outlines of pens, change purses, lipstick cases, headphones and other neat stuff.

Getting Onto The Plane

Memorize your flight number and your seat number.

When you get to your gate, look for the desk that shows your flight number and takeoff time. The agent will tell you how long it will be before you can get on the plane. If you have a few minutes, now is a great time for a bathroom stop. No getting lost in the video arcade or the gift shops!

Listen for the announcements and boarding instructions over the loudspeaker. Stay close to the adults you're flying with as you board the plane. And be sure not to leave any of your things in the boarding area!

If you're flying by yourself

You get to board the plane before everybody else! The airline wants to be sure you're comfortable and buckled in before they let the rest of the herd stampede in.

Listen for the "preboarding announcement" — this means YOU. Say goodbye to whoever brought you to the airport. Then get out your ticket and boarding pass to show to the airline employees at the gate. They'll take you through to find your seat on the plane.

On The Plane

Don't mess with the flight attendant call button.

Getting settled

How to make yourself comfortable for the flight ahead

Where can I put my stuff?

You have two choices: put your bags under the seat in front of you, or in an overhead bin. A bag with things you'll need during the flight belongs under the seat in front of you. If there's no seat in front of you, the flight attendant will help you stow your stuff nearby.

Scope out the plane

Where's the closest bathroom? Where's the closest exit? Where are the controls for your personal air conditioning and personal light? Find your seatbelt and buckle up.

Scope out your neighbors

The people next to you are passengers — not your entertainment. Don't bug them, and don't let them bug you. If your seatmate behaves in a way that makes you uncomfortable, push the flight attendant call button and ask to be moved.

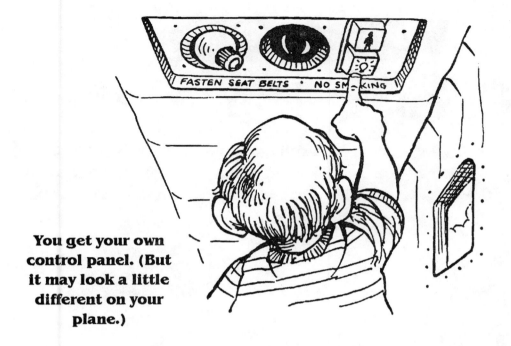

You get your own control panel. (But it may look a little different on your plane.)

When should I call for the attendant?

The only reasons to press the call button during a flight are: if you're scared, if you're hurting, or if somebody won't stop bothering you. On very long flights, you can also buzz if you need something to drink. Please remember the attendants are there for everyone on the plane — don't buzz just because you're bored.

Watch The People Parade!

If you know how to look, being on the plane can provide you with lots of free entertainment. Without being rude and staring, see how many of these people and things you can find as everybody boards the plane. Score 5 points for each one you spot.

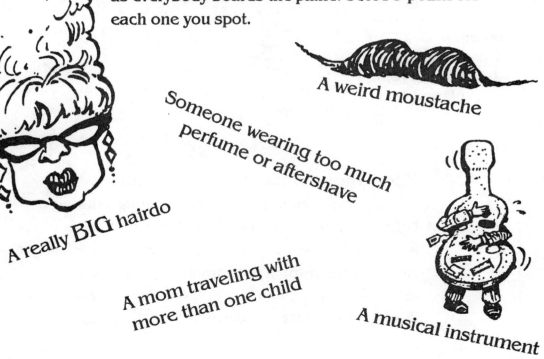

A weird moustache

Someone wearing too much perfume or aftershave

A really BIG hairdo

A mom traveling with more than one child

A musical instrument

A really complicated camera

Really hairy arms

Somebody trying to hide that he's bald

A laptop computer

A tacky outfit

A T-shirt with an **Advertising Slogan** on it

Sports equipment

A personal stereo with headphones

⑩ Point Bonus Question

Look how everybody's dressed. Are there more people on your plane flying for fun, or for business? **My Score** _____

How to be smarter than the grown-ups around you

Listen to the plane's safety announcement — then see how well you score on the Captain's Quiz on the next page.

Some adults behave badly when they're away from home. They act like rules only apply where they come from — but not where they're going.

That's not true, of course. Rules are usually there for a reason, and airplane rules are for your SAFETY. All that stuff they tell you to do — like wear your seatbelt — are to help keep you safe.

Remember, "grown-up" doesn't automatically mean "adult." You might see adults ignoring the flight attendants' safety announcement, not reading the safety card instructions, or not paying attention to the "fasten seatbelt" signs. You might even see them ignoring the request to stay in their seats after the landing.

Be smarter than these grown-ups. Airplanes are built differently, just like cars. Planes may have the same features, but in different places. That's why you need to listen carefully to the safety announcement. But make it fun! Listen to the safety announcement, and then answer the questions on the next page.

Captain Wrightway's Safety Quiz

The correct
answers are on
page 130.

Circle all the correct answers:

1. The captain turns on the lighted over-head signs when he wants you to:

(A) Fasten your seatbelt.

(B) Do the *Hokey Pokey.*

(C) Sing *Jingle Bells.*

2. Your seat cushion is special. Why is that?

(A) It's made from the same fabric as Frazier's couch.

(B) It can float.

(C) When Shaquille O'Neal sits on it, his chin goes between his knees.

3. If you ever need it, an oxygen mask will pop out in front of you. What should you do?

(A) Say, "trick or treat!"

(B) Whip out a crayon and draw kitty whiskers on it.

(C) Strap the mask over your nose and mouth, then gently tug the cord.

BONUS QUESTION — How many rows do you count to the nearest emergency exit?

Name That Noise

Why the plane makes funny noises.

Clomp! Thunk! Whir-r-r-r! What was that? Don't worry. Those are just some of the harmless noises you hear before your plane takes off, and all during your flight.

Here's where all those noises are coming from:

➤ Luggage being loaded into the belly of the plane sounds like *whumps* and *thuds* under the floor.

➤ Air conditioning units can vibrate and *hummm* under your feet.

➤ The covered ramp that connects some planes to the gate *whirrs* away from the door after everybody's on board.

➤ The plane's brakes can *squeal* or *grind* while it's moving on the runway.

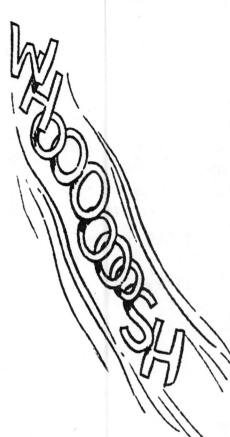

➢ The plane's landing gear goes *clomp* as it locks into position, and *thunk* when it folds back into the plane.

➢ Sometimes the engines get louder on takeoff — and then immediately softer. That's okay. Pilots do that to be quieter as they fly over houses near the airport.

➢ You may hear the wing flaps *flick* or *whirr* into place. If you're sitting near the wings, you may be able to see the flaps go up and down.

➢ The air nozzle over your seat may *hiss*. If it bugs you, reach up and screw it shut.

➢ Normal landings can include *screeches* from the tires, *whines* from the flaps, and a loud engine *roar* as the plane slows down.

Airbumps

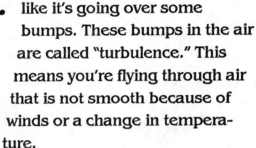

Even though the plane is flying through air, it may feel like it's going over some bumps. These bumps in the air are called "turbulence." This means you're flying through air that is not smooth because of winds or a change in temperature.

You don't have to worry — it happens all the time — and the pilot will steer toward smoother air as soon as possible.

In the meantime...

1. Fasten your seatbelt.
2. Hold onto your drink so it doesn't spill, or drink it up fast.
3. If it's *really* bumpy, make believe you're sitting in the back of the school bus. Or think about a rollercoaster or a horse you've been on. Is this more exciting, or less?

Feeling *Light* & **Heavy**

As the plane takes off, you may feel like you're being pushed back in your seat. You might even feel heavier. That's what's known as the "G-force." It's the same feeling you get in elevators or on roller-coasters when they go up or down very quickly. It's a mild version of what the astronauts feel when the Space Shuttle takes off.

You might also suddenly feel light or floaty in your seat. That's also the G-force. Feeling light or heavy comes from how fast the plane is going, and how quickly it changes altitude (its height off the ground).

Don't worry about this — it's just nature doing what it's supposed to do. In fact, if your seatbelt is securely fastened, pretend you're an astronaut and enjoy it!

What if I'm uncomfortable?

If you're not feeling comfortable, the way to feel better is usually easy and nearby.

Hot?

Turn on your air conditioning. Most planes have a twist-turn air nozzle above your head. If you need help reaching it, ask.

Cold?

Ask the flight attendant for a blanket. Or turn off your air conditioning nozzle.

Hungry?

Get a snack from your busy bag. Or ask the flight attendant for a snack if you don't have anything with you.

Thirsty?

Ask the flight attendant for water or a soft drink.

Light in Your Eyes?

Find the switch and turn off the light above you. If you're in a window seat, close the shade.

Don't Feel Good?

Push the flight attendant call button. Explain what's wrong as best you can. Or turn to page 72 — maybe you can fix it yourself.

How about on the inside?

•••

If you're feeling restless or uncomfortable, there are easy ways to get your mind off it and enjoy the flight.

•••

Nervous?

Adventures are supposed to be a little bit scary. That's why people go to amusement parks. But you don't need to be afraid. Everybody in charge is well-trained and the plane has everything you might NEED. (Things you WANT should come from your busy bag.)

Grumpy?

Are you hungry or tired? A snack or a pillow could help.

Bored?

C'mon, keep reading. Or open that busy bag and take out something fun to do.

Restless?

Try some of the exercises starting on page 74 in this book.

Need to Relax?

Turn to page 80 and take one of the Mental Field Trips.

Captain Wrightway's In-Your-Seat Scavenger Hunt

From your seat, can you see these things, or do you know where they are on your plane?

START

Writing not in English.

Your own light switch.

A movie screen or big TV. (May not be on your plane.)

An airsickness bag. (Barf bag.)

Safety instruction card. (Extra points for reading it!)

Your own air nozzle.

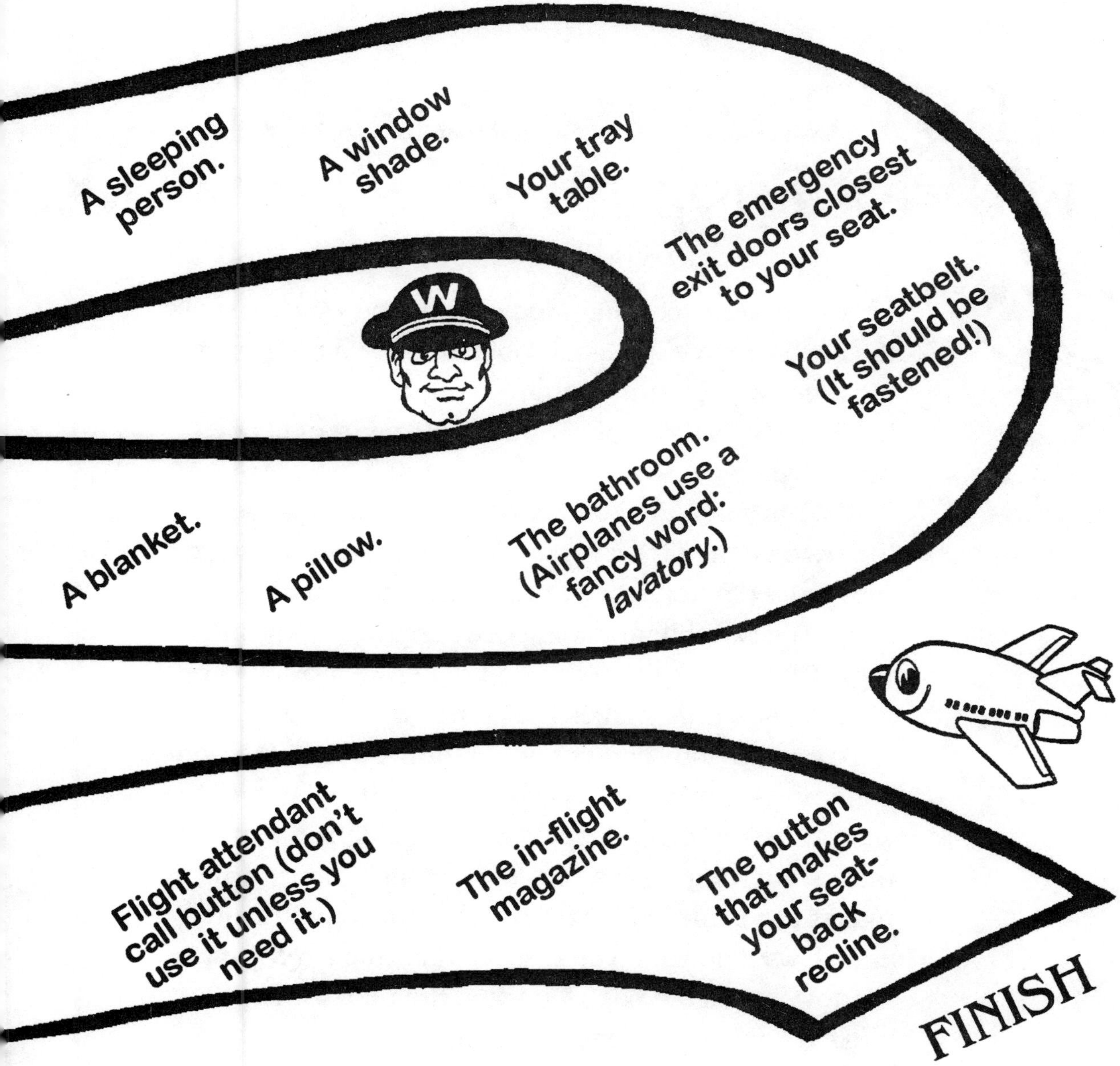

A sleeping person.

A window shade.

Your tray table.

The emergency exit doors closest to your seat.

Your seatbelt. (It should be fastened!)

A blanket.

A pillow.

The bathroom. (Airplanes use a fancy word: *lavatory*.)

Flight attendant call button (don't use it unless you need it.)

The in-flight magazine.

The button that makes your seat-back recline.

FINISH

On The Plane

How does the plane fly without flapping its wings?

Did you ever stick your hand outside the window while the car was moving? Remember how the air felt pushing against your arm? Cupping your hand made it feel like the wind was lifting it away. That's part of why planes can fly.

Airplanes don't need to flap their wings because they're designed to make the air underneath the wing move at a different speed than the air on top of the wing. The two different air speeds create what's called "lift." That makes the plane go up. Engine power — or "thrust" — is what makes the plane go forward.

To change the speed or height of the plane, the pilot controls movable sections that change the shape of the wing. Flipping small flaps up and large flaps down makes the wings less sleek. That creates "drag," which makes the plane work harder to slip through the air, and slows it down. If you can see the wing from your window, watch the flaps flip when the pilot wants to make a change in speed or altitude.

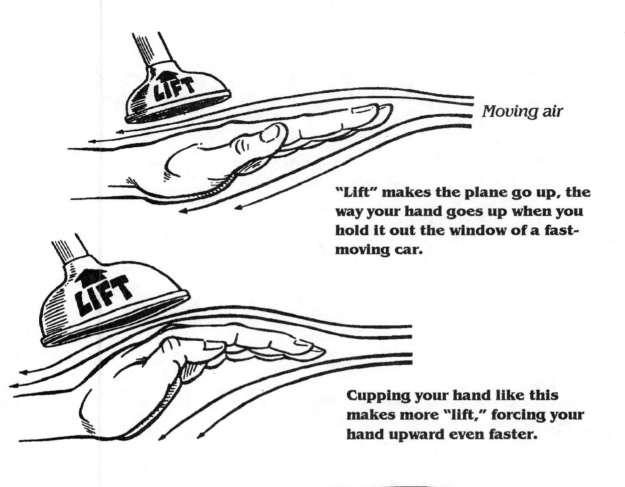

Moving air

"Lift" makes the plane go up, the way your hand goes up when you hold it out the window of a fast-moving car.

Cupping your hand like this makes more "lift," forcing your hand upward even faster.

CROSS SECTION OF WING

Now you know how the wings help lift your plane.

Take apart an airplane

Each of the flaps on the wings are there to help your plane take off, change direction and altitude, or slow down for landing.

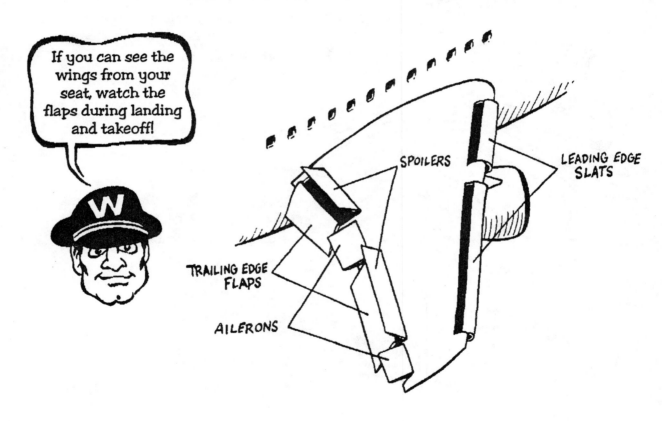

Take apart 'Airplane'

How many words of two or more letters can you find in the word 'AIRPLANE'?

AN   PLAN   _____   _____   _____

_____   _____   _____   _____   _____

_____   _____   _____   _____   _____

_____   _____   _____   _____   _____

_____   _____   _____   _____   _____

Answers on page 130.

Captain Wrightway's Plane Good Manners

The time on a plane is your own. You can work on anything you want, as long as you're not bothering anybody. Captain Wrightway's tips can make the trip better for everybody — especially you.

DO...

✓ Write postcards.
✓ Read.
✓ Watch the movie.
✓ Draw monsters.
✓ Write to a famous person.
✓ Listen to music with head phones.
✓ Sleep if you're tired.
✓ Snack.
✓ Write about your trip in your diary or journal.
✓ Play some games in this book.
✓ Give all your trash to the flight attendant to throw away.
✓ Keep your seatbelt buckled.

BUT...

✗ Don't kick the seat in front of you.
✗ Don't tap on your tray table or flick it open and closed.
✗ Don't play with the window shade.
✗ Don't keep interrupting the person sitting next to you.
✗ Don't walk up and down the aisles for no reason.
✗ Don't drop trash on the floor.
✗ Don't yell or scream.
✗ Don't stick gum under your seat.
✗ Don't play with the reclining seat — find a comfortable position and leave it there.

Tinkle Timing

The aisle on the plane is a one-lane highway that carries traffic in both directions. So when the flight attendants are using the serving cart and blocking the way to the bathroom, it's not the best time to go. Just wait a few minutes for the cart to pass, and then go for it. But if you *REALLY* have to go, don't wait. You can squeeze past the cart, or they'll back it up for you.

You never know when the serving carts will appear. So ask the flight attendant before takeoff for the best time to go up the aisle. (You'll see lots of adults who aren't that smart.) And next time you fly, try to use the bathroom at the airport *BEFORE* you get on the plane.

If the door on the bathroom says, "OCCUPIED," someone's in there. Just wait a minute until it says, "VACANT."

About the world's smallest bathroom

Know your seat number — or count rows — so you can find your seat when you're done!

Even adults get confused about what's what in this teeny airplane bathroom. So here's the scoop on the flying toilet:

➤ Sometimes there's a line of people waiting ahead of you at the bathroom. Be patient.

➤ Once you get in, shut the door and slide the latch so nobody can open the door by mistake. Notice how the latch works, so you can unlatch it easily when you're done.

➤ Don't take all day in there. Others may be waiting.

➤ The sink and toilet aren't the same as yours at home. These are pressurized, so they'll make funny noises.

➤ Water from the sink and what you flush goes into a big tank inside the plane. Machines clean out that tank when the plane gets to the airport.

➤ Don't flush things you shouldn't down the toilet.

➤ If the "Fasten Seat Belt" sign comes on while you're in there, just finish what you're doing and go back to your seat.

Outside Your Window

Real life that's better than television!

The Clouds Below

Some of the most exciting things you'll see on a plane take place outside your window. You can take off on a dark, rainy day — and within minutes — you can fly into bright sunshine and clear blue skies.

That's because your plane flies above the weather happening on the ground. The clouds are giant weather clues — if you know how to read them.

Clouds are made up of tiny ice crystals or water droplets. They're formed by moving air and changes in temperature and altitude. We can't see through them, but a pilot's instruments can.

Clouds come in all shapes and sizes. They fall into several categories, which make them easy to identify.

Cirrus Clouds

Cirrus *(seer'-us)* clouds are the highest kind. They look like feathery white streaks in the cold air above 20,000 feet. They're made of ice crystals carried by winds blowing at different speeds. When a faster wind picks up the biggest part of the cloud, the rest of the cloud trails behind. They're called "mares' tails," because they're shaped like horses' tails.

Stratus Clouds

You've seen stratus *(strat'-us)* clouds from the ground. They look like a low grey ceiling, and often produce fog or drizzle. Stratus clouds are made of tiny water droplets. As your plane flies up past these clouds into clear, sunny skies, stratus clouds may block your view of the ground for a while. But don't worry, it's still there.

Cumulus Clouds

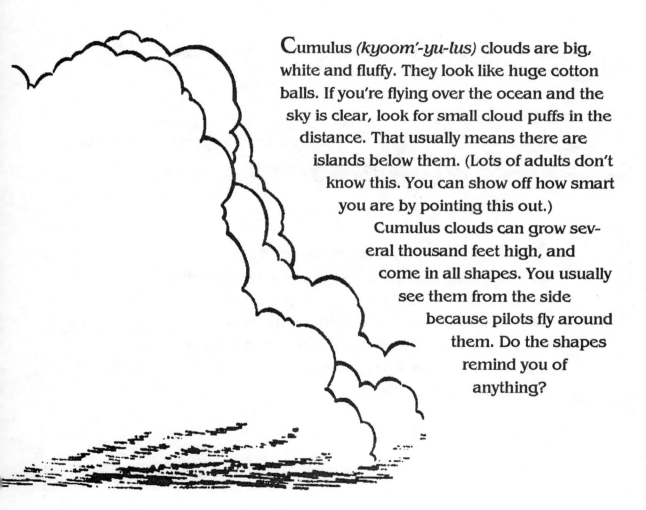

Cumulus *(kyoom'-yu-lus)* clouds are big, white and fluffy. They look like huge cotton balls. If you're flying over the ocean and the sky is clear, look for small cloud puffs in the distance. That usually means there are islands below them. (Lots of adults don't know this. You can show off how smart you are by pointing this out.)

Cumulus clouds can grow several thousand feet high, and come in all shapes. You usually see them from the side because pilots fly around them. Do the shapes remind you of anything?

Fog

Have you ever walked through fog in the morning? That's what it would feel like if you could walk through a cloud. From your plane, you may see fog alongside mountains and near ocean shorelines. It forms on the ground when cold wet air flows into warmer places. In deep valleys during cold weather, fog can become more than 1,000 feet thick!

Smoke

If you see a lot of smoke coming from one area on the ground, you may be getting a bird's eye view of a fire. You can even tell the wind direction by which way the smoke is blowing.

Smog

You've heard about air pollution — now you can see how this dirty air hangs over a city. During takeoff and landing, look for a flat layer of brownish fog. Even though smog makes colorful sunrises and sunsets, it's bad for the environment. Smog is made of pollution from cars, factories and even planes.

Round Rainbows

Rainbows happen when light rays are separated into color bands by moisture droplets in the air. On the ground, you can see arch-shaped rainbows when the sun is at your back and rain is falling in another part of the sky. Rainbows look like half-circles, because the ground keeps us from seeing the rest of the arch beyond the horizon. But in the air, there's no ground to stop you from seeing the whole rainbow — so, if the conditions are right, you might see a *round* rainbow from your plane window.

Glowing Glories

If you are sitting on the side of the plane away from the sun, and you can see the plane's shadow on the clouds below you, look for a ring of colored light around the plane's shadow. That's called a "glory." If you're very high above the clouds, you might not even see the plane's shadow, just the glory. They happen because the moisture droplets bend the sunlight, separating it into colored bands. The scientific name for this is "refraction," but most people just say, *"Ooooh."*

The AMAZING REAL-LIFE NATURE MOVING Picture Show

Get ready to learn a lot about the area you're flying over when you see it from the air!

Mountains

Are you flying over mountains? Are they sharp and rocky, or soft-looking and green? "New" mountains are rocky and have fewer trees and plants — they haven't been around long enough for the weather to erode the rocks into topsoil. Without enough topsoil, plants and trees can't grow. The Rocky Mountains are newer mountains — somewhere between 70 and 250 million years old (that's young, in earth terms). Softer mountains wearing carpets of plants can be 600 million years old or more. On the east coast, the Adirondacks, Appalachians, Berkshires and Blue Ridge Mountains have all been worn down by weather, so they look soft and green in the summer.

Look for tree lines on high mountains. A tree line marks the highest point where trees can grow because the weather becomes too harsh for them.

Rivers

Flying over a river? You can tell whether it's an older or newer river by how twisty it is. If you see big loops in the river's course, it's an older river and probably flows pretty slowly. Younger rivers move in straighter lines, because the water rushes faster through the riverbed. If you're flying during the dry season, it may be harder to spot the river from the plane window, but there are still clues to help you find the riverbed. Look for the towns, cities and clumps of trees usually found along a river's edge.

Desert

If you're flying over the desert, look for faint dark wavy lines that are either roads or dry riverbeds — sometimes both. If the area has a rainy season, the beds carry flood runoff. When that happens, local residents on the ground are warned not to use those roads!

Farmland

Farmland is different in different parts of the country. Flying over the Great Plains and Midwest, farms look pretty square — except for the big circles in the middle of some squares. Those circles are crops watered by systems that rotate from the center, making round fields. East of the Mississippi River the farms can be odd-shaped, because earlier ways of measuring out land made sure everybody got a piece of the riverbank.

Flying At Night

If you're flying at night, it's easy to see where people live and how big their cities are. After families have turned out their lights and gone to bed, you'll still see lights in towns and cities coming from cars, street lights, power plants and advertising signs.

Captain Wrightway's Outside-The-Window Scavenger Hunt

From your seat, how many of these things can you see outside your window?

HINT: Watch for some of these things after takeoff and before landing. They may be too small to see when you're too high in the air.

START

Your plane's shadow on the ground.

A river.

Cumulus clouds. (See page 58)

An island.

A lake.

Skyscrapers.

A reservoir.

Smog. (See page 59)

Swimming pools.

A baseball field.

Cirrus clouds.
(See page 56)

Another airport.

A power plant.

A "glory."
(see page 60)

A church.

Cloud shadows on the ground.

A highway.

Other plane's jet streams.

Your plane's shadow on cloud-tops.

FINISH

On The Plane

How come 3 hours on the plane is 6 hours later?

Be sure to change your watch if you need to!

Before clocks, people told time by the sun. We still do. Because the earth is round and turning, the sun is always rising or setting someplace.

If all the people in the world set their watches to the same time, some people would have to eat lunch in the dark and go to bed when the sun came up, so that people on the other side of the planet could have their meals and bedtimes at the usual times.

So, in 1883, everybody got together and agreed to divide the globe into 24 sections (24 hours, get it?). That way, you get to do daytime things in daylight. And Aunt Minnie gets to sleep and eat at the right times, too, even though her city might be two or three hours ahead of you (or behind you) on the clock.

Time zones are why it's 8:21 in New York when it's 7:21 in Chicago, 6:21 in Denver and 5:21 in Los Angeles. Everybody uses the same minutes; all they change is the hours.

Turn to the map at the back of the in-flight magazine, or look at this map, and notice where the time

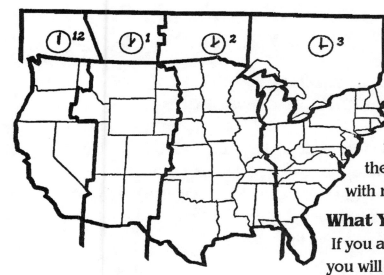

zones change. The lines aren't exactly straight, because people living in cities along the time-change lines chose which of the two time zones they wanted. Look for states in the U.S. (and provinces in Canada) with more than one time zone.

What YOU need to do

If you are flying across time zone lines, you will need to adjust your watch when you land, so you're on the same time as everybody around you. If you have a question about whether to change your watch earlier or later, ask.

It's easy to change your watch, but your body might take a little while to figure out why supper is at a different time. And the first night, you might not be sleepy at bedtime. This is called "jet lag." The best thing to do is to go with the LOCAL time — if the people at your destination are having lunch, you eat, too. Just do what they're doing and give your body a chance to catch up.

Where am I on the map?

Pretend you're the navigator and chart your own flight.

First, look in the seat pocket for the airline's in-flight magazine. Toward the back of the magazine, you should find maps showing the major cities where your airline flies. Ask for help if you can't find the magazine, or your destination on the map.

The Quick Way

1. With a pen or pencil, draw a line from where you're starting your flight to where you're ending your flight.
2. Ask the flight attendant how long the entire flight should take. Write it here: ____.
3. What time did you actually take off? ____.
4. On the magazine map, use a pen or pencil to divide your trip line into four equal sections.
5. When you have flown one-fourth of the flight in time, you have flown about one-fourth of the trip in distance. Mark it on the map — that's about where you are. Which state or province are you now flying over?

The Tricky Way

Mark all you want in the in-flight magazine. It's yours to keep!

Ask the flight attendant what is the distance of your trip in miles, and what is the plane's average crusing speed in miles per hour?

DISTANCE _____   AVERAGE CRUISING SPEED _____

1. Write the time the plane took off: _____.
2. Write down what time it is now: _____.
3. Count how many minutes you've been flying: _____ (Remember, each hour has 60 minutes.)
4. Divide the average cruising speed of your trip by 60 for the miles-per-minute you are traveling: _____.
5. Now multiply your answer from #3 by your answer from #4, and write it here: _____. This will tell you about how many miles you've flown so far.
6. In the back of your in-flight magazine, find the map of your plane's route. Draw a line from the starting point of your flight to the ending point.
7. Check the map scale (if it has one) to see how many miles equals one inch. Now you can figure out how many inches you've flown and you'll know where you are on the map.
8. If you've figured all this out, you're a hot shot. Ever thought about becoming a navigator?

Upset Stomach? Get a grip on yourself!

For thousands of years, before doctors and drugstores, Chinese people knew how to spell relief: A-C-U-P-R-E-S-S-U-R-E. Since you're buckled in your seat, far from a pharmacy, take a tip from the Chinese if your stomach gets fluttery.

There's a place on your arm that calms down your stomach when you press it. If you're wearing long sleeves, roll them up. First, feel the bend inside your left elbow with your right thumb. Above that spot, you can feel where your muscle starts (see the illustration at right). Put two fingers at the bottom of that muscle. Now press that spot hard, but not so hard that it hurts. Breathe in and out slowly, three times, and then stop pressing.

You can repeat this as many times as you want. Soon, you'll notice your stomach feeling better. You might even notice your mouth isn't so dry anymore.

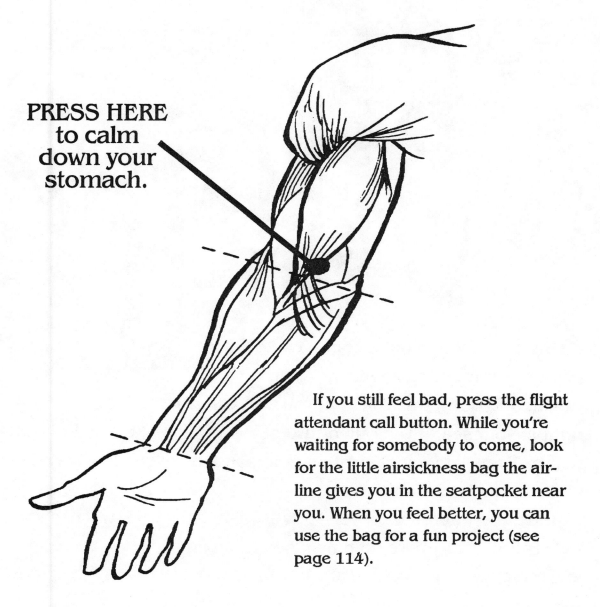

PRESS HERE to calm down your stomach.

If you still feel bad, press the flight attendant call button. While you're waiting for somebody to come, look for the little airsickness bag the airline gives you in the seatpocket near you. When you feel better, you can use the bag for a fun project (see page 114).

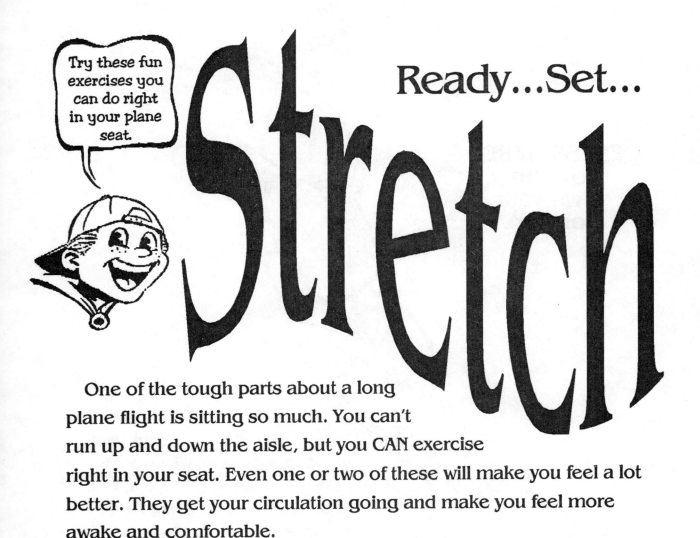

Try these fun exercises you can do right in your plane seat.

Ready...Set...

Stretch

One of the tough parts about a long plane flight is sitting so much. You can't run up and down the aisle, but you CAN exercise right in your seat. Even one or two of these will make you feel a lot better. They get your circulation going and make you feel more awake and comfortable.

Don't worry about what you look like. Anybody who watches you will realize what you're doing, and might even copy you because it feels so good. Just flip up your tray table and give it a try!

The Bigfoot Air Shuffle

Even if your feet don't reach the floor, pretend you're driving the Flintstones' car and 'walk' the plane for a minute or two. Be careful not to kick the seat in front of you.

Now make little circles with your feet, turning them at your ankles. Then do the same thing with your hands and wrists.

The Mega-NO

Keeping your shoulders down, turn your chin to your right shoulder, then s-l-o-w-l-y turn your chin to your left shoulder. Now go back to the right. Now the left again. Do this at least ten times. Doesn't that feel good?

The Hugga-Hugga

Give yourself a hug! Wrap your arms around yourself, then quickly twist yourself around to the left, then all the way around to the right, then back to the left again. Repeat five times each way.

The "I Dunno"

Shrug like you would if somebody asked, "Who broke this?"

Slowly bring your shoulders up to your ears, then lower them as far as they'll go. Feels pretty good, huh? So do it again.

The Elephant Ear Flap

Clasp your hands behind your head and pull your elbows back toward the seat. Feel your shoulder blades squeeze together? Relax and do it again. Be sure not to wing the person sitting next to you.

Mental Field Trips

Aren't you smart! You brought something wonderful to play with on the plane, and you didn't even have to pack it. It's your imagination. In your mind, you can go anyplace and do anything. Taking a Mental Field Trip will help you pass the time and perk you up. So choose a daydream and let's go!

Mental Field Trip #1

Sit up straight, uncross your legs, close your eyes and relax your hands in your lap.

Now picture your favorite superhero's headquarters. In your mind, walk there. Imagine all the things you might see on the way to meeting someone like Superman or the Power Rangers. Give yourself a few superpowers of your own, in case you run into any villains or monsters.

In your mind, you'll see the headquarters get bigger as you get closer. Once you get there, plan your next adventure with your superhero. Draw a picture of what the two of you plan:

Mental Field Trip #2

Your brain is like a VCR. Since you're sitting for a while, pick out your own "memory movie" and replay it inside your head. Gently close your eyes, sit up straight, and let your arms and legs relax completely.

Now think of a time you felt really, REALLY good. Maybe it was after you won a prize, or a time you made somebody you love feel very happy. Pick that memory, replay it in your mind, and enjoy the nice feelings all over again. Draw your favorite scene from your "memory movie:"

REC   PLAY

#3 Close your eyes and pretend you're a beautiful happy gold kite, easily and silently floating on a breeze. See how you sparkle in the sunlight. Now imagine your trip, high and fast enough to have the sky to yourself, low and slow enough to see all the great sights. Enjoy floating over everything. (It's all right if you fall asleep — that's REALLY relaxed!) When you wake up, write down all the things you "saw" in your mind while you were a kite!

. . . .

#4 Take a penny and squish it between your thumb and forefinger. Either hand is fine. Hold your breath and squeeze as hard as you can — count to 5 — THEN relax. Notice how nice and loose your hand feels. Imagine sending that feeling up that arm, across your shoulders, and down the other arm. Try it with your other hand.

What's The Deal With

My Ears?

You might feel pressure or little 'pops' in your ears as you take off or land. It's not dangerous, it just feels weird.

Remember your manners — cover your yawns!

Inside your head, your ears are connected to your nose and your throat. When the air pressure OUT-SIDE your ears is different than the air pressure INSIDE, your ear drums aren't sure what to do. The difference in air pressure inside the plane during takeoff and landing gets in the way of your hearing, and also feels a little strange.

What you can do

The quickest way to make the air pressure the same on both sides of your ear drums is to yawn. Even if you're not sleepy, go ahead and yawn a few times and notice the pops.

Another way to make your ears feel normal again is to chew gum. That makes your jaws go up and down, which works almost the same as yawning. Actually, any chewing works pretty well. If you have carrot sticks in your busy bag, you can snack and pop at the same time!

Landing: How to be smarter than grown-ups

As you get close to your destination, the pilot prepares the plane for landing. Your ears may feel funny, and you might hear *clunks* and *whirrs* as the pilot moves the landing gear into place. This is good — it means everything's working exactly right.

The 'Fasten Seatbelt' light goes on, and the flight attendants make one last trip down the aisle to collect your trash.

This is the time when you can really be smarter than the grown-ups around you. Enjoy watching how skillfully the pilots land the plane on the runway. But remember — just because you've landed doesn't mean you're ready to get off the plane!

The plane has to 'taxi,' or ride down the runway to the airport terminal. The flight attendants ask everybody to stay in their seats with their seatbelts on, until the plane reaches the terminal. You may see bone-headed adults ignoring this safety rule. You be smarter!

Watch out when someone opens the overhead bins! Stuff can move around in there during the flight and land on your head!

By jumping up and pushing, those people will get where they're going a whole 60 seconds before you — not worth it for ignoring safety rules!

Also, stuff in the overhead bins sometimes shifts during the flight. Anybody who opens the bins while the plane is moving could get a big conk on the head! The rule about staying buckled in is a safety rule. Please follow it.

Once the plane stops moving, and the flight attendants signal it's okay to go, undo your safety belt and do a quick check:

The Last-Second Before-Leaving-The-Plane Quick Check

➢ Where's my ticket?
➢ Am I leaving with all the bags I brought onto the plane?
➢ Did I bring a coat or sweater?
➢ Did I put anything in an overhead bin?
➢ Is there anything of mine under the seat in front of me?
➢ Do I want to take the free magazine?
➢ Am I forgetting anything?

Flying Freebies

Most airlines offer some freebies to well-behaved passengers who are smart enough to ask for them. If the flight attendants didn't already hand them to you, wait for a time when they're not busy and ask if there are any kid-things the airline gives away. Depending on which airline you're flying, there could be:

➤ free soft drinks
➤ an in-flight magazine (it's okay to take it with you)
➤ a deck of cards
➤ postcards
➤ coloring books (usually for littler kids, but ask anyway)
➤ pencils
➤ souvenir flight pins
➤ other assorted doodads

Remember to say thanks!

Airport Smarts

Captain Wrightway's Tips on Airport Navigation

Back on the ground, people are pushing and rushing again. They either want to collect their bags and go, or rush to another gate where a "connecting flight" will take them on the next part of their trip. Don't get confused or upset by the rushing — know what YOU need to do, and do it.

Need a bathroom? Tell the person with you.

Any bags you checked onto the plane need a few minutes to get from the airplane to the baggage area. Don't worry, you don't have to rush. Your bags will wait for you. Just follow the signs that say 'Baggage Claim.'

If you are traveling alone

...and you are meeting somebody

If you don't see the person who was supposed to meet you, don't get upset. The airline person looking out for you can arrange a phone call. Get the number, and call to let them know you're here now. If there's no answer, they're probably on the way and stuck in traffic. The airline person won't leave you until you're picked up. Hang in there.

...and you have a connecting flight

If you need to connect to another airplane, the person escorting you has all your information.

If your plane was delayed and you can't make your connection, don't worry. The airline will let you call the person who's supposed to meet you. Together, you can all figure out what's best to do.

If you have extra time, and you want to look around, ask the agent at the gate how long before your flight boards. Together, agree on how much time you have for exploring. Then, check your watch often so you can make your plane on time.

Different City — Same Rules

When you're waiting, the best place for your carry-on and busy bag is on the floor between your feet.

Airports look so much alike that you might not feel like you're in a new city yet. But there is one way this airport is just like the one where your trip started: you need to be alert and smart about how you handle yourself and your stuff.

➢ Be self-responsible! Use your Maximum Maturity Mode.

➢ Stay with the people you know. Don't talk to strangers and don't let them talk to you.

➢ Remember why you're there — don't be distracted by stores, food or video arcades.

➢ Even if you feel tired or crabby, use your best intelligence and maturity. It makes things easier for you AND the people around you.

➢ Don't let any strangers hand you anything to hold for them.

➢ If you get lost, go right up to the nearest airline counter and tell the person behind the desk. You don't have to wait in the line.

If you're going through Customs

If you travel outside your own country, expect to go through extra steps at the airport. They may check what country you're from, whether you're carrying plants or fruit, and you'll go through Customs.

The Customs Service keeps people from bringing dangerous things into the country, and to make sure people pay taxes on goodies they bought in other countries. It's their job to find out what you've got with you, and sometimes even to go through your stuff.

Be polite and honest when the customs officer asks you questions. Some kids worry if they have something very personal in their luggage, like a blanket or a favorite doll. Don't worry, the customs officers don't care — that's not what they're looking for.

Bag-O-Rama

If you checked any bags at the first airport, now you'll get them back.

After your plane lands, luggage handlers quickly unload everyone's bags from the plane and send them into the terminal. You'll soon find your bags with everyone else's in the baggage claim area.

Some baggage systems look like moving belts. Others look like carnival rides. BUT THEY'RE NOT! They are designed only for bags. It is VERY DANGEROUS for people. Your bag comes to you, so just pick a place to stand and watch for yours.

See how many bags look alike? That's why you were smart to put on name tags and stickers to make your bag stand out from the others. If you want it to be even easier on your next trip, think up a bright design you can make on your bag with colored plastic tape.

Watch out for careless people swinging their bags off the carousel. Don't get bopped!

What you need to do

An airport security guard may ask to see your baggage claim ticket before you leave the area. You should find it stapled to your airplane ticket, so have it ready to show him.

If your bag is open or broken, tell the person you're with RIGHT AWAY. Both of you can check to see that everything's still there. If something's missing, or if the bag is damaged, both of you should go to the Baggage Claim Office immediately and file a report.

If your bag hasn't shown up and everyone else's luggage has been picked up, ask the person you're with to check if all the luggage is off the plane. Both of you should go immediately to the Baggage Claim Office and file a report. Even if they tell you that your bag is coming on the next flight, file the report anyway. With a report on file, the airline will deliver your bag to you once it shows up.

Become A People-ologist

Now that you're in a new city, look for how the people are the same — and different — from the people in the city you left.

Listen for accents and regional words

In different cities, a submarine sandwich may be called a "sub," "hero," "hoagie" or "grinder." If you ask for a "soda," some parts of the country will give you a drink made with ice cream; in other cities, "soda" means "pop," a carbonated soft drink. In various places, the underground trains are called "the subway", "the Metro," "BART," "the tube" or "the underground."

Look to see if they dress differently

If it's winter and you're flying from a cold city to a warm one, seeing shorts in December can be a surprise! Are most people wearing business clothes or play clothes? Do you see more cowboy boots or jogging shoes? Do people wear hats in this part of the country?

Be alert for different smells

Is a good-smelling flower blooming in this city? Do they cook different foods? Can you smell the salt water of an ocean, or the fishing industry on a river? Does some local factory give this city its own aroma?

Listen for any special local music

Some areas are tied to certain kinds of music — Country, Jazz, Latin, Rap, New Age, Grunge Rock, Blues, etc. Some cities are known for their symphonies. But don't worry, MTV will be exactly the same.

Bag Yourself A Design

A good luggage design is bright, colorful and special. That's how you can spot your bag among a bunch of other bags. Try out some designs here:

What will you use to make these designs on your suit-case?

Be sure to ask for permission before putting anything on the actual suitcase!

If I Owned The Airline

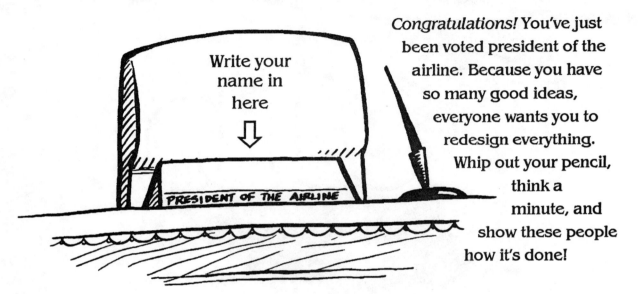

Write your name in here
⬇

PRESIDENT OF THE AIRLINE

Congratulations! You've just been voted president of the airline. Because you have so many good ideas, everyone wants you to redesign everything. Whip out your pencil, think a minute, and show these people how it's done!

What'll we call your airline?

(You can call it anything that isn't already being used.)

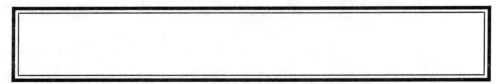

What's the
new symbol?

This is the little picture that makes everybody think of your company. It's called a "logo" (low'-go). Go ahead and decorate this plane with your new logo.

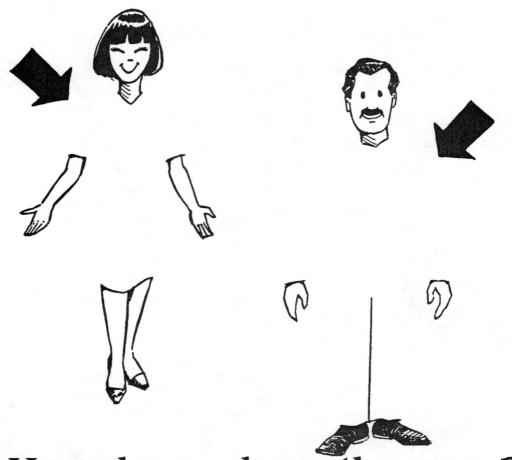

How do we dress the crew?

Give the flight crew new uniforms.
Use your imagination, so they don't look too much
like Star Trek or the Mighty Morphin Power Rangers.

What'll we feed the passengers?

Who says airplane food has to be peanuts or mystery meat?
You've got the pencil, you're the boss.
Cook up something wonderful to serve on your planes!

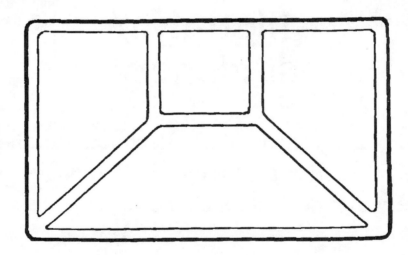

LOOK!
Your very own high-flyin' stationery.

Airplane rides are the perfect time to write short notes to friends. Use the next few pages for your very own designer stationery.

What do you like best about this book?

Write us a note on your new stationery and send it to:
CorkScrew Press, 4470 Sunset Blvd.
Suite 234, Los Angeles, CA 90027

A note from 32,000 feet!

Dear _____,

REAL AIR MAIL

Captain's Log
JOURNAL ENTRY

Date _____

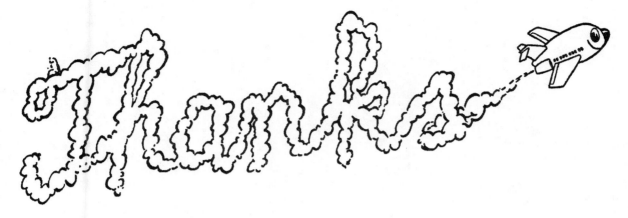

Dear _____,

Secret Words

Circle the words hidden in this box.
They can be read up, down, across or diagonally

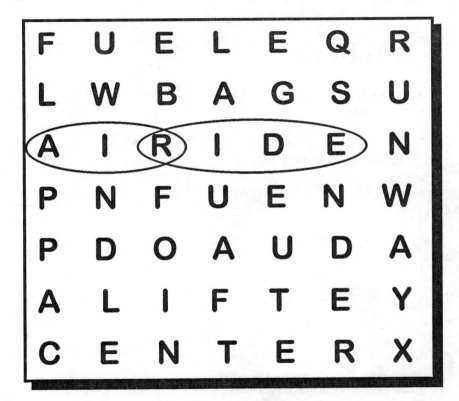

F	U	E	L	E	Q	R
L	W	B	A	G	S	U
A	I	R	I	D	E	N
P	N	F	U	E	N	W
P	D	O	A	U	D	A
A	L	I	F	T	E	Y
C	E	N	T	E	R	X

Words to find: air, ride, wind, flap, lift, earn, runway, pal, fun, clouds, edge, fat, bags, fig, sender, center, fuel, aft, awe.
For the answers, see page 131.

Things You Wish You Could See...

...Outside The Window

Now draw your own! ⇨

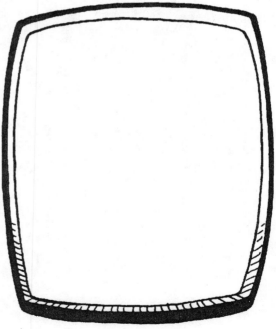

The Do-It-Yourself, In-Your-Seat Hand Puppet

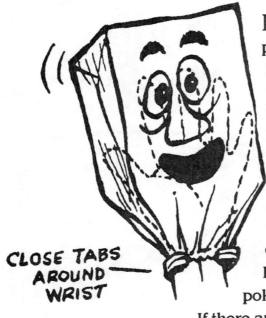

CLOSE TABS AROUND WRIST

In the seat pocket in front of you is a hand puppet just waiting for you to set him free. Right now, he looks like a square, boring barf bag — your creativity and a little artwork can transform him into Chuck, your secret silly airplane buddy.

Reach in and bring him out, and give him a face. You can draw him just like the cartoon on the next page, or improve him by making him more like a dragon or a superhero.

Be careful while you're drawing — don't poke through the face.

If there are other littler kids sitting near you on the plane, you can do a good deed by giving a small show. Make them laugh! Later, you can take your puppet with you when you leave the plane.

Crossword Puzzle #1

Clues

Across

1 World War I flying _ _ _
5 Where the planes are
6 Something to play with
8 H_2O

Down

2 Assistant plane flyer
3 What makes the plane fly (see page 46)
4 What slows the plane down (see page 46)
6 The thing that shows your bag is yours
7 Are you having fun yet?

Answers on page 131.

Crossword Puzzle #2

Clues

Across

1 What you say when you find something
5 To get into the sky, the plane takes _ _ _
7 Getting there
8 Abbreviation for New York's time zone in winter
9 A game where nobody's winning yet
10 Babies of America's national bird
13 Crossing time zones can give you jet _ _ _ (page 69)
14 Planes and birds need them to fly
15 Bear's bedroom or lion's home
16 When someone's proud of you, she _ _ _ _ _

Down

2 Benjamin Franklin says it makes waste
3 Something beautiful
4 If you're in the air, what you're in
5 Breakfast food: _ _ _meal
6 How the plane gets to Cleveland
11 A flying machine with no engine
12 Christmas drink

Answers on page 131.

Write the Wright Brothers

Since you already know how to connect the dots, we're using this space to tell you about the first flight.

Two bicycle-building brothers from Dayton, Ohio were crazy about flying. In 1903, no one had done it yet, except for some Europeans in hot-air balloons. But Wilbur and Orville Wright were determined to be famous for something besides their weird names. So after many experiments with kites, gliders and bicycles with flaps, they built a double-winged machine with a gasoline engine. They took their machine to Kitty Hawk, North Carolina to try it out. (Did you connect the dots yet?)

Orville lay face down on the bottom wing. Wilbur released the plane, and his brother took the first engine-powered manned flight in history. It lasted an entire 12 seconds, and took him a whole 120 feet. But Wilbur and Orville proved to the world that heavier-than-air machines COULD fly.

Progress has made lots of improvements on planes since 1903. Aircraft are no longer bi-planes, and you can fly sitting up.

In-Flight Origami

Since you're spending some time in the air, you might as well solve some of life's major questions.

Make yourself a fortune teller — just don't make the people around you crazy with your new talent.

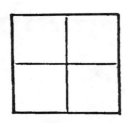

INSTRUCTIONS

1. Carefully tear out the next page.
2. Fold the page in half longways and crossways, to make creases. Then open it up again.

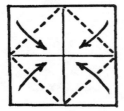

3. With the four fortunes facing down, fold all four corners into the center
4. Turn the page over.

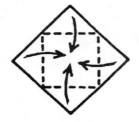

5. Now fold each of the corners into the center again.

continued on page 125

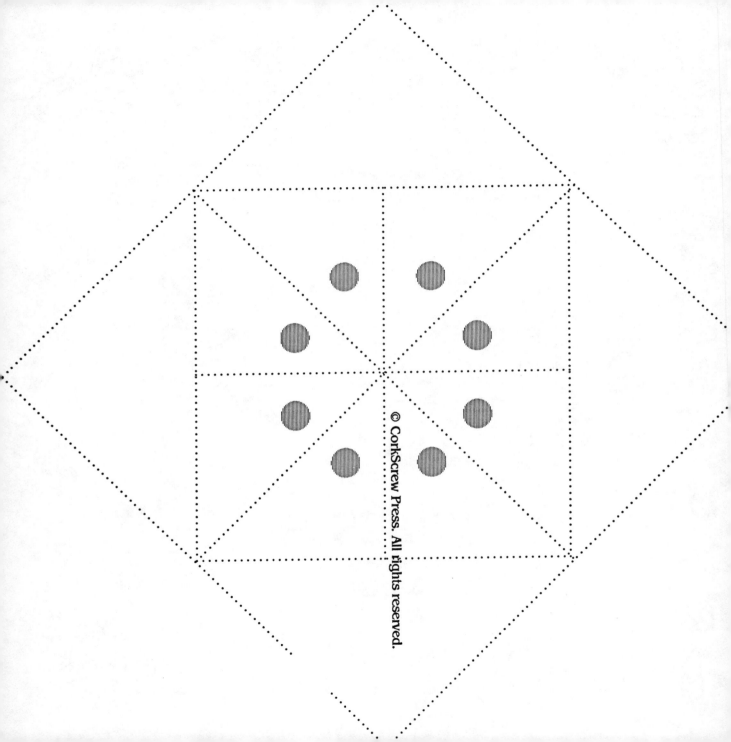

Origami continued

6. Turn the page over again so the planes are facing you.

7. Fold the square in half to make a rectangle, with two planes on each side.

8. With the planes facing up, slip your thumbs and first fingers under the planes, and pinch them all together to make a point in the center.

9. Keeping your thumbs together and your first fingers together, push your thumbs against each other and away from your fingers. Surprise!

10. Close them back to the center, and move the right side away from the left side. Surprise!

☞ Ask yourself a question that can be answered 'yes' or 'no.' Spell out your name, moving the fortune teller back and forth with each letter. When you finish your name, reach into the center and pull up ONE flap. The underside holds your answer.

Now you're ready to tell fortunes, and give brilliant answers to any yes-or-no question.

Autographs!

Who's on this plane with you?

Date _____ Flight Number _____

From _____ To _____

If they're not too busy, and you ask politely, maybe the
flight attendants can get the pilots to autograph your book for you!

> **Pilot**

> **Co-pilot**

> **Flight Attendant**

Flight Attendant

Fellow Passenger

Fellow Passenger

Famous Person

How was your trip?

1. What was the best thing about the flight? Why?

2. What was the favorite thing you learned?

3. The next time I fly, I want to

4. I would like to fly to _____.
   Draw a picture.

Answer Key

From page 20

Everything but Number 3 gets a big $. Wouldn't it be great if Number 3 were true?

From page 21

1. Man carrying too much, can't see where he's going.
2. Someone left luggage where it is easy to trip over.
3. Man sleeping, not watching his belongings.
4. Man leaving expensive camera unguarded.
5. Man careless with airline ticket.
6. Money easy to take from pocket.
7. Money and ticket not zipped inside backpack.
8. Mom not watching purse and leaving it open.
9. Lady not watching present.
10 No ID tag on man's duffel bag.

Answer Key

From page 37

1-A   Fasten your seatbelt. The only way the Hokey Pokey counts is if you put your whole self in, and buckle up.

2-B   It can float. The Shaq's chin is ALWAYS between his knees when he sits down.

3-C   Strap the mask over your nose and mouth, then gently tug the cord. No tricks; the treat is oxygen when you need it.

From page 49

in	pi	pa	ail	pen	per
rip	air	pal	lip	are	ape
pea	pie	pin	par	lap	rap
ran	nap	nip	era	plan	area
pane	pale	near	lear	line	rile
Nile	nail	lira	pail	pile	nape
rail	pine	lair	line	pain	leap
reap	pair	lane	ripe	pear	peal
real	pare	pier	arena	learn	plain
ripen	plane	Nepal	pearl	panel	April
peril	alien	Alpine	*Can you find more?*		

From page 111

There are also lots of little words inside bigger words. Did you see them, too?

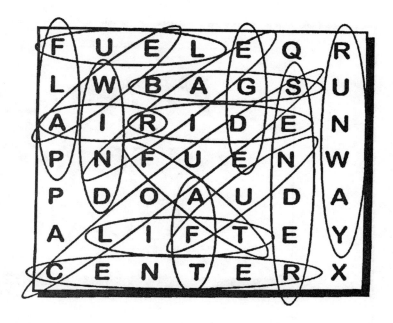

<table>
<tr><td>F</td><td>U</td><td>E</td><td>L</td><td>E</td><td>Q</td><td>R</td></tr>
<tr><td>L</td><td>W</td><td>B</td><td>A</td><td>G</td><td>S</td><td>U</td></tr>
<tr><td>A</td><td>I</td><td>R</td><td>I</td><td>D</td><td>E</td><td>N</td></tr>
<tr><td>P</td><td>N</td><td>F</td><td>U</td><td>E</td><td>N</td><td>W</td></tr>
<tr><td>P</td><td>D</td><td>O</td><td>A</td><td>U</td><td>D</td><td>A</td></tr>
<tr><td>A</td><td>L</td><td>I</td><td>F</td><td>T</td><td>E</td><td>Y</td></tr>
<tr><td>C</td><td>E</td><td>N</td><td>T</td><td>E</td><td>R</td><td>X</td></tr>
</table>

From Page 116

Across	Down
1 Ace	2 Copilot
5 Airport	3 Lift
6 Toy	4 Drag
8 Water	6 Tag
	7 Yes

From Page 118

Across		Down
1 Aha	10 Eaglets	2 Haste
5 Off	13 Lag	3 Art
7 Arrival	14 Wings	4 Airplane
8 Est	15 Den	5 Oat
9 Tie	16 Brags	6 Flies
		11 Glider
		12 Eggnog

Parent's Resource Guide

Children may be a joy, but traveling with the little blessings is infinitely more complicated than traveling alone. Whether the current crisis is needing a tissue at 32,000 feet — or an unexpected six-hour layover in a strange airport — planning, common sense and preparation will make the trip much easier.

This resource guide for parents is designed to coordinate with the children's section. Please read both, so you can know what your child may expect, and how best to help him or her.

KEY

☆ Children flying alone.

◆ All children, whether flying alone, escorted or with a parent.

Is Your Child Flying Alone?

You will learn the true meaning of, "Some things are harder to watch than to do." Look for the starred sections (☆) for special insights and extra help. Then congratulate your child for his or her bravery — and congratulate yourself for doing a fine job of launching such a capable kid!

Age Requirements

☆ If your child is at least five years old, he can fly alone on a domestic flight — if there is no change of planes.

☆ If your child is between eight and eleven years old, and there IS a change of planes, he will need an escort between planes. Some airlines charge for this. Call and ask.

☆ If your child is twelve or older, he is allowed to make connecting flights alone, although you can still arrange for an escort (and you may have to pay a fee.)

◆ If you need to fly with a baby, call the airline AND your pediatrician. Toddlers may be held on your lap, but safety seats are preferable if you can afford the extra fare. Some airlines rent safety seats — others may let you use your own car-safety seat. Call the airline and ask.

☆ The rules among international carriers differ for children flying alone. Call each airline you plan to use.

◆ Make sure your child is old enough for this experience — not just meeting the airlines' age requirement — but emotionally advanced enough to feel confident and comfortable on the flight.

Airline Reservations & Ticketing

♦ Call the airline to learn its requirements and recommendations for flying with children. Ask if there are any special discount fares for kids traveling with adults.

☆ Tell the reservation agent that your child will be an "unaccompanied minor" and give the child's age.

♦ Try to book a "nonstop" flight. A "direct" flight will include one or more stops — with extra waiting time.

♦ If possible, plan your travel for times and seasons with the least possibility of delay. Your child will be less restless — and you'll worry less — when there is less chance of snow delays, crowded airports or overbooked flights. The agent can advise you on which flights are least crowded.

♦ If your child is taking this book on the plane, ask for a window seat — some activities require a window view.

♦ Need more legroom? Ask for seats in the "bulkhead" (the first seats in any section of the plane). You'll have to stow all your carry-on bags in the overhead bin, but you may be closer to the restrooms.

♦ If your child flies a lot, start a frequent flyer account for him and start racking up mileage and free flights!

Slip-Up Insurance

☆ **Fill out and make several photocopies of the *Flying Fact Sheet* on the inside front cover of this book.** Place a copy in each piece of luggage, each carry-on bag and in the child's pocket. Make an extra copy for yourself — this gives you a complete itinerary all in one place, and should answer most questions. Be sure to include the ticket's serial number: if the ticket is lost, this will help the airline to speed up ticket replacement.

◆ Write down the names of everyone you deal with, from the travel professional through the reservation agent. This will help make confirmations easier later on.

☆ Although most airlines watch for this, NEVER schedule a child for the last connecting flight of the day. This avoids an overnight stay if the flight is cancelled.

Advance Planning

◆ With enough notice, airlines that provide food can give your child a special kids' meal. Most airlines can place this order as late as 24-hours ahead, but don't depend on the food service — be sure your child is carrying snacks he'll eat.

◆ If your child requires any special medicine or treatment, check with your pediatrician. Children with asthma, diabetes or other conditions can be affected by climate or time changes. They may need to take special precautions.

◆ Be sure your own carry-on bag contains any medications you or your child need, as well as an extra pair of eyeglasses and copies of all eyeglass prescriptions. Never pack these items in your luggage!

☆ If you have concerns about the person who will meet your child at the other end of the trip, consider mailing or faxing a copy of page 142 of this Parent's Resource Guide, along with the Flying Fact Sheet on the inside front cover.

◆ Schedule your return a couple of days before school or work begins, to give your bodies time to readjust.

International Flying

◆ Be sure each adult and child brings proof of nationality — usually a passport or birth certificate and photo ID.

☆ Provide your child with pocket change in the currency of the destination country, for phone calls or emergencies.

◆ A minor flying without his parents should always carry written authorization from BOTH his parents. This technicality can cause an unpleasant surprise for grandparents, just moments before takeoff.

◆ In the case of divorce, a parent may need to show divorce and custody papers when flying with a child. If you are the parent who <u>does not</u> have custody, you may also need to show notarized permission from the parent who does. If a parent is deceased, you may need to show a death certificate. If you do not have the same last name as your child, you may need to show a photocopied birth certificate to prove your relationship. In all cases, requirements vary by country (and sometimes by the hour). It is strongly recommended that you check with each country's tourism office in advance of your trip.

Rehearse Your Child

◆ Make sure your child understands appropriate behavior towards strangers, and how to avoid trouble. If your child gets lost, or needs immediate help, tell him he can go to any airline ticket counter — and that he needn't wait in line. Review pages 18-19.

☆ Make sure your child knows how to place a collect call, and knows his own area code and phone number.

☆ Make sure your child is up to the responsibility of carrying money and his plane ticket. See page 20 for tips on carrying money safely.

◆ For younger children, set aside practice playtimes that are the same duration as the flight. Praise the child for amusing himself and/or behaving for that length of time. For instance, "If we got on an airplane at the same time you started playing, we'd be in Atlanta by now."

◆ Practice airport navigation by taking a field trip to the airport on a day when you have no flight to catch. Seeing and knowing the terminal will help your child feel more comfortable and form more realistic expectations.

Emotional Preparation

◆ Attitudes are contagious. Approach this trip as a positive adventure. Your child will pick up your concerns or anxieties, even if you don't voice them.

◆ Listen to your child's fears. The news media bring scary information and images into your living room. If your child worries about crashing or being kidnapped, discuss this at his level. Don't dismiss his concerns. What ISN'T discussed can often be scarier than the truth.

Preparing a Carry-On Busy Bag

◆ Get a backpack or canvas bookbag big enough to hold toys and snacks, yet small enough to be carried easily and fit under the airline seat. At least one zipper compartment is recommended for pocket change and phone numbers. Compartments inside the bag are ideal for the plane ticket. Remind your child NOT to carry folding money or the plane ticket in an external pocket of a backpack.

◆ Tag the busy bag with the child's last name and the phone number to return the bag if it's lost. Don't use the child's first name on the tag or on external clothing, so no stranger can say, "Come here, *Andy!*"

◆ Begin collecting interesting surprises for an in-flight busy bag. You might even postpone buying a desired toy, so it can be included with in-flight goodies.

☆ Personal notes, gift-wrapped surprises and treats will add warmth to your child's trip and emotional well-being.

◆ Snacks like non-messy fruit, juice boxes and sandwiches will ensure he doesn't get cranky because he is hungry.

◆ Little ears feel pressure changes even more strongly. Be sure to provide chewing gum or carrot sticks for ear-pops.

◆ Make sure your child's carry-on bag includes a toothbrush, toothpaste and one change of clothing, in case his checked baggage is delayed.

☆ Make sure your child carries all his medications, eyeglasses, and a copy of his eyeglass prescription.

☆ Remember, the airline's job is to transport your child, not to babysit or entertain him. Be sure you've included sufficient activities and snacks in the busy bag.

Good Busy Bag Choices

• Self-contained creative travel-sized toys without a lot of pieces, like Magna-doodle or Travel Etch-A-Sketch.
• Personal stereo WITH headphones.
• Wrapped nonperishable snacks, like individual cheeses, dry cereal or apple slices in moisture-lock bags.
• Crayons or markers in packages of 8-24.
• Paper for drawing and writing.

Bad Busy Bag Choices

• "One-trick" toys that quickly become boring.
• Toy guns won't even make it past Airport Security.
• Toys with lots of little pieces or sound effects.
• Messy foods.

Before You Leave The House

• Plan to check-in at the gate 60 to 90 minutes before takeoff to allow for traffic, parking, check-in and tantrums. Not needing to rush lessens your child's anxiety and the pressure on you — and gives time for proper good-byes.
☆ Figure on an extra half-hour to fill out the unaccompanied minor paperwork. Waiting time after check-in can be spent sitting and talking over a soft drink or ice cream cone.
☆ Call the person who will be picking up your child, to get

the **actual** number where he'll be during the time of the flight. A work number is no good if your contact is out of the office and your child's flight is delayed.

☆ Make sure your child has money for an emergency, plus anything you want him to be able to buy. Twenty dollars in fives and ones is much more useful than a twenty-dollar bill. Have him divide the money into several hiding places: phone-call coins in a pocket, folding spending money in a pocket with a flap, and larger bills hidden in a secret place, possibly a sock or shoe.

☆ Make sure your child memorizes the city and airport he's flying to, and who will pick him up.

◆ Dress your child in loose, easy-to-change clothing and comfortable shoes. Dressing the child in layers of clothing makes it easier to adjust to different in-flight temperatures.

◆ Check the current weather at your destination. Pack an umbrella or warmer clothes, if necessary.

At The Airport

☆ If the gates are restricted to passengers, you'll need to get a pass at the check-in counter so they'll allow you to walk the child to the gate. Bring identification with you.

☆ Unaccompanied minors board first. Watch the time so you don't lose this advantage. You may be allowed to accompany your child on board to help him get settled in.

☆ Introduce your child to the airline's gate agent, and ask that he or she introduce your child to the flight crew. Make sure your child knows that these are the people he should approach if he has a problem.

☆ Do not leave the airport until the child's plane is *in the air,* in case the aircraft has to return to the terminal. Make certain no prior appointments will pull you away from the airport until any takeoff delays have been handled.

☆ The airline can refuse to board an unaccompanied minor if bad weather threatens to divert his flight.

On The Plane

◆ Hand-held computer games and personal stereos are great, but not during takeoffs or landings. Be sure your child understands this is a safety rule, and must not be disobeyed.

◆ Be sure your child understands that visits to see the cockpit and meet the pilot are permitted only if the pilot agrees, and only when the plane is on the ground. You can ask the flight attendant to check if she can arrange a visit at the end of the flight.

◆ Children are more prone to ear problems on a plane than adults. To unclog ears during descent, have the child swallow vigorously, yawn widely or chew gum. Not sleeping during descent can help, since your child must be awake to try these methods. If ear pain persists for 12 hours or more after a flight, consult a doctor.

If You Are Picking Up An Unescorted Child At The Airport

☆ Arrive at the gate early. Few traumas are more heart-rending to a child than that abandoned feeling when nobody is waiting. This delay also puts pressure on airline personnel, who have to console the child while trying to locate you.

☆ When you arrive at the gate, tell airline personnel the name of the unescorted minor you are picking up.

☆ If you must be late, call the airline. They can have an employee watch your child until you get there.

☆ You must be the person listed on the Unaccompanied Minor form. Bring an identification card that shows your photo. Airline personnel are not permitted to release the child just because you seem to know him (or he seems to know you). Pitching a scene because you've left your ID in the car sets a bad example and upsets everyone. Don't just dash in expecting to pick up the kid on the run. Respect the rules and appreciate that airline personnel are protecting your child by doing their jobs.

☆ Make a quick call the people who dropped off the child at the beginning of the trip to let them know everything's okay.

When is the last time you got your parents a gift they *REALLY* used?

	How Many?	Price Each		Total Price
✓ ***How To Fly: Relaxed & Happy From Takeoff To Touchdown*** — for adults who don't like to fly.	_____	x $5.95	=	_____
✓ ***The Safe Tourist*** — Hundreds of tips on how to protect your family from vacation dangers.	_____	x $6.95	=	_____
✓ ***How To Fly — For Kids!*** More copies for friends, cousins and going-away gifts.	_____	x $8.95	=	_____

NAME	Book Total _____
ADDRESS APT. NO.	6% Sales Tax (CT addresses only) _____
CITY STATE ZIP	Subtotal _____
DAYTIME PHONE NUMBER WITH AREA CODE ( )	S&H ($3 per book) _____
	Order Total _____

Mail orders: Complete the charge card information at right or enclose check or money order payable to: *Globe Pequot Press.* Mail to: P.O. Box 833, Old Saybrook, CT 06475-0833.

Fax orders: Fax this form day or night with your credit card information: **203/395-0312**

Charge It! 1-800-243-0495

☐ MasterCard ☐ VISA

Card Number _____

Expiration Date (mo/yr) _____

Signature _____

In Connecticut call toll-free: **1-800-962-0973**

In A Hurry? Overnight or 2-day *RUSH* delivery is available for a small extra charge on phone orders only. **Call 1-800-243-0495.**

10-Day Money-Back Guarantee if not completely satisfied.

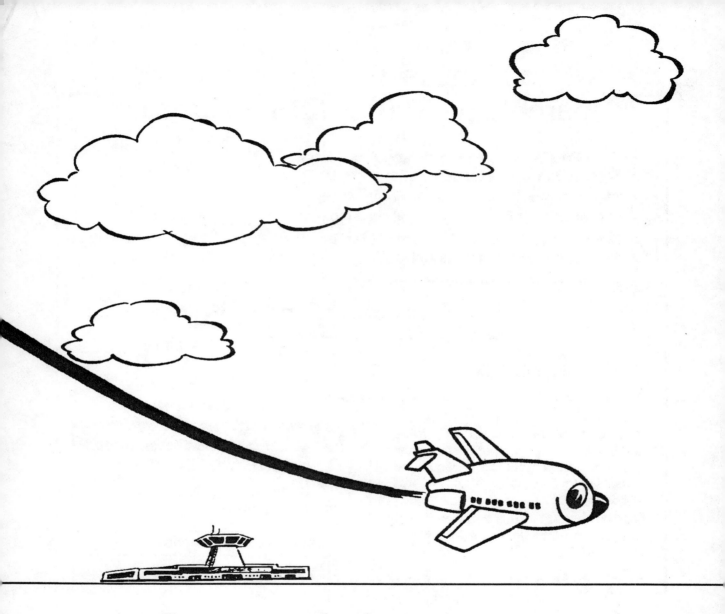

Congratulations on your excellent airplane adventure!